Adapted by Stefano Ambrosio

Artwork by Giovanni Rigano
Igor Chimisso
Silvano Scolari
Andrea Cagol
Stefano Attardi
Carlotta Quattrocolo
Marco Ghiglione
Alessandro Ferrari
Kawaii Creative Studio

Based on the screenplay written by Ted Elliott & Terry Rossio
Based on characters created by Ted Elliott & Terry Rossio
and Stuart Beattie and Jay Wolpert
Based on Walt Disney's Pirates of the Caribbean
Produced by Jerry Bruckheimer
Directed by Gore Verbinski

DISNEP
PRESS

New York

Printed in the United States of America
First U.S. Edition
1 3 5 7 9 10 8 6 4 2
Library of Congress Catalog Card Number 2007903438
ISBN-13: 978-1-4231-0449-0
ISBN-10: 1-4231-0449-8

WHAT MAKES YOU THINK I NEED PROTECTION?

YOUR MASTER, **SAO FENG**, IS EXPECTING US. HE HAS PROMISED US SAFE PASSAGE.

BUT A SMART PIRATE ALWAYS HAS AN ALTERNATIVE ESCAPE ROUTE. . .

. . . SO THE CREW OF THE **BLACK PEARL** SECRETLY FILE THROUGH A GRATE. . .

RASP RASP

. . . THE NOISE COVERED BY A CART DRAWN BY THE MYSTIC, **TIA DALMA**.

MEANWHILE, ELIZABETH AND BARBOSSA HAVE REACHED SAO FENG'S LAIR.

CAPTAIN SAO FENG, THANK YOU FOR GRANTING ME THIS AUDIENCE. I'VE A **VENTURE** UNDER WAY, AND I'M IN NEED OF A SHIP AND A CREW. . .

HUH. THAT'S AN ODD **COINCIDENCE!**

YOU CAN *FIGHT!* YOU ARE SAO FENG, THE PIRATE LORD OF SINGAPORE. YOU COMMAND IN THE *AGE OF PIRACY.* WOULD YOU HAVE THAT ERA COME TO AN END ON YOUR WATCH?

LIZABETH SWANN, THERE IS MORE TO YOU THAN MEETS THE EYE. BUT YOU HAVE FAILED TO ANSWER MY QUESTION. . .

WHAT IS IT YOU SEEK IN DAVY JONES'S LOCKER, IN THE WORLD BEYOND THIS ONE?

JACK SPARROW! HE'S ONE OF THE PIRATE LORDS!

HE HELD ONE OF THE NINE *PIECES OF EIGHT!*

HE FAILED TO PASS IT ALONG TO A SUCCESSOR BEFORE HE *DIED.* AND SO WE MUST GO AND FETCH HIM BA—

GET YOUR WEAPONS! THERE'S A *TRAITOR* AMONG US!

BUT SAO FENG HAS NOTICED THAT THE *TATTOO* ON THE GUARD'S ARM IS *FAKE!*

GIBBS AND HIS CREW HAVE BEEN LYING IN WAIT BELOW SAO FENG'S LAIR. NOW THEY QUICKLY PUSH *SWORDS* THROUGH THE FLOORBOARDS FOR BARBOSSA AND ELIZABETH.

7

THE *TRAITOR* BELONGS TO THE EAST INDIA TRADING COMPANY, WHOSE AGENTS, LED BY *MERCER*, COME STORMING IN EVEN NOW . . .

. . . AS BELOW, GIBBS AND THE REST OF THE *BLACK PEARL'S* CREW WASTE NO TIME SETTING OFF *EXPLOSIVES* TO CREATE AN *ESCAPE ROUTE* THROUGH THE TUNNELS.

VERY SOON, THE *DUTCHMAN*, NOW THE SCOURGE OF ALL PIRATES, IS HAILED BY THE *ENDEAVOUR*.

INSIDE THE *ENDEAVOUR*, LORD *CUTLER BECKETT* IS TROUBLED BY MERCER'S REPORT OF THE RECENT EVENTS IN *SINGAPORE*.

SO THE *BRETHREN COURT* HAS BEEN CALLED. WHERE DO THEY MEET? TO WHAT PURPOSE? WHAT HAPPENS WHEN THE NINE PIECES OF EIGHT ARE BROUGHT TOGETHER?

MEANWHILE, ON THE *FLYING DUTCHMAN*, DAVY JONES IS PONDERING WHAT HE HAS BECOME.

ONCE HIS FATE WAS TO FERRY THOSE WHO DIED AT SEA FROM THIS WORLD TO THE NEXT. HE WAS CHARGED WITH THIS DUTY BY THE *SEA GODDESS CALYPSO* . . .

. . . NOW HE *EXTERMINATES* PIRATES, AS COMMANDED BY THE *COMPANY!*

TU-TUMP

AND HE CANNOT REFUSE, SINCE BECKETT POSSESSES THE *DEAD MAN'S CHEST* CONTAINING JONES'S *STILL-BEATING HEART!*

11

THE SUN BURNS OVER *DAVY JONES'S LOCKER...*

I DON'T SEE JACK. I DON'T SEE *ANYONE.*

WITTY JACK BE CLOSER THAN YOU THINK.

JACK ARRIVES, ABOARD THE *BLACK PEARL* — CARRIED BY *MILLIONS OF CRABS!*

WILL! GIBBS! WHERE HAVE YOU BEEN? WERE YOU KILLED BY THE *KRAKEN?* OR SOMETHING ELSE? SOMETHING *PAINFUL,* I HOPE—

BARBOSSA!

JACK, JACK, GET OVER HERE! WE CAME TO *RESCUE* YOU.

JACK, LISTEN. *CUTLER BECKETT* HAS THE HEART OF DAVY JONES. HE *CONTROLS* THE *FLYING DUTCHMAN.*

HE'S TAKING OVER THE *SEAS!*

THE SONG HAS BEEN SUNG. THE BRETHREN COURT IS *CALLED.*

AYE, JACK. THE WORLD NEEDS YOU BACK SOMETHING *FIERCE!*

WHY SHOULD I SAIL WITH ANY OF YOU? FOUR OF YOU HAVE TRIED TO KILL ME IN THE PAST. . .

ONE OF YOU *SUCCEEDED.*

?!

SHE HASN'T TOLD YOU? THEN YOU'LL HAVE LOTS TO TALK ABOUT.

ONCE EVERYONE IS ABOARD THE *PEARL,* THE VOYAGE BACK BEGINS. . .

14

LATER. . .

THE *BLACK PEARL* IS STILL SAILING TOWARD THE "WORLD OF THE LIVING" WHEN ITS CREW SEES A STRANGE SIGHT.

YOUCH!

THEY ARE THE UNFORTUNATE SOULS WHO HAVE DIED AT SEA, FINDING THEIR OWN WAY TO THE "OTHER SIDE." ONCE THEY WOULD HAVE BEEN *FERRIED* BY DAVY JONES. . .

THAT WAS THE DUTY HE WAS CHARGED WITH BY THE GODDESS CALYPSO. AND *EVERY TEN YEARS*, HE COULD COME ASHORE, TO BE WITH SHE WHO LOVED HIM TRULY. . . BUT HE HAS BECOME A *MONSTER!*

M-MY FATHER?

ELIZABETH. . .

16

THE BLACK PEARL ROCKS COMPLETELY OVER INTO THE WATER. . .

AS THE RIDDLE SPOKE: "OVER THE EDGE, BACK, OVER AGAIN. . ."

"...FLASH OF GREEN!"

AND FINALLY THEY SAIL ONCE AGAIN IN THE *REAL SEA*, IN THE WORLD OF THE LIVING!

WE'RE BACK!

THIS WAS YOUR IDEA, AND THE FACT THAT I WENT ALONG DOES NOT MAKE YOU ANY LESS STUPID!

NOW IT'S TIME TO GO TO *SHIPWRECK COVE*. BUT...

RIGHT NOW, WE NEED WATER. THE CHARTS SHOW AN *ISLAND* NEARBY WITH A WATER SPRING!

WILL PERSUADES BARBOSSA AND JACK TO GO ASHORE TOGETHER... BUT THE ISLAND IS FULL OF SURPRISES. FIRST THEY FIND THE *KRAKEN*, DAVY JONES'S MONSTROUS PET, *DEAD!*

I BET FOLK WOULD PAY A SHILLING TO SEE THIS!

HEY—WHAT...

SURPRISE NUMBER TWO: WILL *BETRAYED* ALL OF THEM! HE CHOSE THAT ISLAND NOT FOR THE WATER...

...BUT BECAUSE *SAO FENG* WAS WAITING THERE ON HIS FIGHTING SHIP, THE *EMPRESS!*

OUTNUMBERED, THE *PEARL'S* CREW ARE TAKEN PRISONER.

AND IT SEEMS SAO FENG HAS AN AXE TO GRIND.

JACK SPARROW. YOU PAID ME GREAT INSULT, ONCE!

SLAP

20

WHY DIDN'T YOU TELL ME YOU WERE PLANNING THIS?

IT WAS *MY BURDEN* TO BEAR.

JACK, THERE'S AN *OLD FRIEND* WHO WANTS TO SEE YOU.

!

JACK IS DISMAYED TO RECOGNIZE *BECKETT'S* SHIP, THE *ENDEAVOUR!*

LATER, IN BECKETT'S CABIN...

REMARKABLE. WHEN LAST I SAW THE *BLACK PEARL*, IT WAS ON FIRE AND *SINKING* BENEATH THE WAVES...

CLOSE YOUR EYES AND PRETEND IT'S ALL A BAD DREAM. THAT'S HOW I GET BY.

JACK'S BANTER COVERS HIS REAL PURPOSE—SEARCHING THE ROOM FOR DAVY JONES'S HEART...

...BUT JACK ISN'T THE ONLY SMART MAN ON THE SEA!

YOU CAN STOP *SEARCHING*, JACK. IT'S NOT *HERE!*

21

MEANWHILE, ON THE *BLACK PEARL*, THERE IS MORE BETRAYAL AFOOT: MERCER PROMISED SAO FENG THE *PEARL*, AND SAO FENG PROMISED IT TO WILL—BUT NEITHER OF THEM UPHELD THEIR BARGAIN, AND NOW. . .

. . . MERCER IS TAKING CONTROL OF THE SHIP!

YOU AGREED, THE *BLACK PEARL* WAS TO BE *MINE*.

BECKETT AGREED, THE *BLACK PEARL* WAS TO BE *MINE*.

LORD BECKETT WOULDN'T GIVE UP THE *ONE* SHIP AS MIGHT PROVE A MATCH FOR THE *DUTCHMAN*, WOULD HE?

AS MUCH AS SAO FENG HATES KNUCKLING UNDER, HE SEES LITTLE CHOICE. THE PIRATES, EVEN UNITED, STAND NO CHANCE AGAINST THE COMPANY.

BETTER TO MAKE PEACE WITH THE COMPANY THAN FIGHT A DOOMED BATTLE.

THEY HAVE THE *DUTCHMAN*. AND WHAT DO THE BRETHREN HAVE?

WE HAVE. . . *CALYPSO!*

SUDDENLY, THINGS DON'T LOOK SO DIRE FOR THE PIRATES' SIDE. SAO FENG BEGINS TO RECONSIDER.

23

JACK NEEDS TO GET BACK ON THE **BLACK PEARL**...

SO HE AIMS A CANNON AT THE **ENDEAVOUR'S** MAST...

BLAAAM

SWOOOOOSH

...AND USES THE FORCE OF THE CANNON'S RECOIL TO FLING HIMSELF BACK ONTO HIS SHIP!

TELL ME YOU DIDN'T MISS ME.

BACK ON THE **ENDEAVOUR**...

·SIGNAL THE **DUTCHMAN!** THEY WILL HUNT THE **EMPRESS** WHILE WE FOLLOW THE **PEARL**... HOW SOON CAN WE HAVE THE SHIP READY TO PURSUE?

THERE'S NO TIME TO ANSWER: THE MAST THAT WAS HIT BY JACK'S CANNONBALL CRACKS AND FALLS!

CREEEAKK

THE *EMPRESS* AND THE *BLACK PEARL* EACH SAIL TO SHIPWRECK COVE FOLLOWING A DIFFERENT COURSE...

ON THE *EMPRESS*, ELIZABETH IS HELD PRISONER BY SAO FENG, WHO BELIEVES SHE IS *CALYPSO*.

...THE FIRST BRETHREN COURT BOUND YOU IN *HUMAN FORM*.

BUT SUDDENLY...

CRASH

THE FLYING DUTCHMAN ATTACKS!

TAKE THE CAPTAIN'S KNOT. GO IN MY PLACE TO SHIPWRECK COVE... *CALYPSO.*

ELIZABETH, NOW A *PIRATE LORD* AND THE CAPTAIN OF THE *EMPRESS*, STEPS ONTO THE DECK, JUST IN TIME TO SEE *DAVY JONES'S CREW* SWARMING ONTO THE *EMPRESS*...

...AND TO FIND *NORRINGTON* LEADING THE ATTACK!

JAMES?

ELIZABETH!

YOUR *FATHER* WILL BE OVERJOYED TO KNOW YOU ARE WELL.

MY FATHER IS *DEAD!*

NO, HE'S NOT. HE RETURNED TO ENGLAND.

LORD BECKETT TOLD YOU THAT?

. . . YES.

AS HE SAYS IT, NORRINGTON REALIZES THAT BECKETT LIED TO HIM!

ELIZABETH IS HELD CAPTIVE IN THE *FLYING DUTCHMAN'S* BRIG.

THERE, SHE FINALLY MEETS *BOOTSTRAP BILL,* WILL'S FATHER. . . DOOMED TO BE PART OF DAVY JONES'S CREW FOREVER!

ELIZABETH AND THE CHINESE PIRATES ARE CAPTURED.

WILL IS ALIVE, AND. . . HE WANTS TO HELP YOU.

HE CAN'T SAVE ME. HE WON'T. BECAUSE OF YOU.

IF JONES BE SLAIN. . . HE WHO SLAYS HIM TAKES HIS PLACE. CAPTAIN. *FOREVER.*

IF WILL SAVES ME. . . HE LOSES *YOU.*

THE NEXT MORNING. . .

SOMEONE ON THE *PEARL* HAS BEEN LEAVING A TRAIL OF FLOATING BODIES FOR THE *ENDEAVOUR* TO FOLLOW. . .

A BETRAYER AMONG THEM?

A GAMBIT! ADJUST COURSE, LIEUTENANT.

SIR!

. . . AND THE BETRAYER ON THE *PEARL* IS *WILL!*

HMM. . . WHAT YOU INTEND TO DO, ONCE YOU'VE GIVEN UP THE LOCATION OF THE BRETHREN COURT?

ASK BECKETT TO FREE MY FATHER!

BUT JACK HAS A *VERY DIFFERENT* PLAN. SO. . .

?!

BE SURE TO GIVE DAVY JONES MY REGARDS!

SOCK

28

LATER, THE SAME NIGHT...

WILL HAS BEEN RESCUED BY THE *ENDEAVOUR* AND NOW...

BARBOSSA HAS SUMMONED THE BRETHREN COURT FOR A PURPOSE. TO FREE SOMEONE NAMED CALYPSO.

CALYPSO! NO... THEY CAN'T. THE BRETHREN WERE TO KEEP HER IMPRISONED FOREVER... THAT WAS THE AGREEMENT...

WILL FINALLY FIGURES OUT THE TRUTH.

YOU TOLD THE FIRST COURT HOW TO BIND HER! AND THAT'S WHY YOU CUT OUT YOUR HEART!

WE MUST STOP THEM! SHE WILL DESTROY US ALL!

THEN IT IS MORE IMPERATIVE THAN EVER THAT WE FIND THE BRETHREN COURT. HOW WILL WE FIND THEM NOW?

THE ANSWER IS IN WILL'S HANDS: THE *MAGIC COMPASS* POINTS TO WHAT YOU WANT MOST. BECKETT WANTS JACK, JACK HAS JOINED THE BRETHREN...

I WANT YOUR ASSURANCE: ELIZABETH WILL NOT BE HARMED. AND MY FATHER GOES FREE!

...SO BECKETT WILL FIND THE BRETHREN THROUGH HIS DESIRE TO KILL JACK.

MEANWHILE... THE **BRETHREN COURT** HAS GATHERED. ALL NINE PIRATE LORDS IN ONE PLACE!

MISTRESS CHING FROM THE PACIFIC OCEAN

AMMAND THE CORSAIR FROM THE BARBARY COAST

AS HE WHO ISSUED SUMMONS, I CONVENE THIS, THE **FOURTH** BRETHREN COURT!

SRI SUMBHAJEE FROM THE INDIAN OCEAN

BOOOM BOOOH

CAPTAIN VILLANUEVA FROM SPAIN

CAPTAIN BARBOSSA

CAPITAINE CHEVALLE, THE ARISTOCRATIC FRENCHMAN

CAPTAIN JACK SPARROW

GENTLEMAN JOCARD, A SLAVE TURNED PIRATE

AND **CAPTAIN ELIZABETH SWANN!**

THE FIRST **COURT** CAPTURED THE **SEA GODDESS.** THAT WAS A MISTAKE. WE OPENED THE DOOR FOR BECKETT AND HIS ILK.

GENTLEMEN, LADIES... WE MUST **FREE** CALYPSO!

MEANWHILE, *TIA DALMA* IS VISITED BY DAVY JONES. . .

YOU. . . HAVE COME TO *KILL* ME BEFORE THE BRETHREN SET ME FREE?

THE BRETHREN'S SPELL SHOULD HAVE STRIPPED YOU OF YOUR MEMORY. . . *CALYPSO!*

IT CAME BACK SLOWLY. . . AND WITH IT, SOME SMALL PORTION OF *MY POWER.* ENOUGH TO REKINDLE LIFE IN BARBOSSA.

LOOK WHAT YOU HAVE BROUGHT UPON YOURSELF. YOU'VE NEVER BEEN A MONSTER, NEVER *CRUEL!*

AS TIA DALMA TOUCHES JONES, HE'S *TRANSFORMED BACK* TO HIS HUMAN FORM. . .

. . BUT ONLY FOR A BRIEF MOMENT!

I DON'T LOVE YOU!

I LEARNED IT FROM YOU! TEN YEARS I LABORED, DISPATCHING THE DUTY YOU ASSIGNED ME, BUT WHEN THE TIME CAME TO STEP ASHORE. . . YOU WEREN'T THERE! *WHY?*

IT'S MY NATURE. BUT I MAY HAVE BEEN THERE THE NEXT TIME. WOULD YOU LOVE ME IF I WAS ANYTHING BUT WHAT I AM?

THAT'S A SHAME, BECAUSE WHEN I AM SET FREE, I WOULD GIVE YOU *MY HEART*. . .

. . .AND WE WOULD BE TOGETHER, IF ONLY *YOU* HAD A HEART TO GIVE!

33

THE ENEMY IS INDEED HERE. . . AND THE ENEMY HAS A GARGANTUAN ARMADA, LED BY THE TWO FIERCEST SHIPS ON THE SEA, THE *ENDEAVOUR* AND THE *FLYING DUTCHMAN.*

PARLAY?

THE PIRATE CREW LOOKS TO JACK—

SO IT'S TIME TO TRY BARGAINING TO AVOID A WAR, BUT. . .

WILL! YOU BE THE CUR THAT LED THESE WOLVES TO OUR DOOR!

DON'T BLAME HIM, BARBOSSA! IF YOU WISH TO SEE THE *ARCHITECT* OF THE BETRAYAL, LOOK AT SPARROW!

ME?

MY ACTIONS WERE MY OWN, TO MY OWN PURPOSE. . . TO *FREE MY FATHER!*

WILL, I SAW YOUR FATHER ON THE DUTCHMAN. . . BUT I FEAR IT IS A LOST CAUSE.

WELL, "KING," ADVISE YOUR BRETHREN: YOU CAN FIGHT, AND **ALL OF YOU** WILL DIE. OR YOU CAN **NOT** FIGHT AND ONLY **MOST** OF YOU WILL DIE.

BECKETT, YOU MURDERED MY FATHER. WE WILL FIGHT. . . AND SURELY **YOU** WILL DIE!

THE DICE IS CAST AND THE SCORE IS **WAR!** BUT AS THEY WALK AWAY. . .

JACK'S **PIECE OF EIGHT**, WHICH HAD DROPPED ONTO THE SAND, IS PICKED UP BY BARBOSSA. . .

. . . WHO NEEDS ALL NINE "PIECES OF EIGHT" TO CAST THE SPELL THAT WILL FREE CALYPSO!

IS THERE AN INCANTATION?

AYE, WE MUST SPEAK THE WORDS. . .

EVEN RAGETTI'S WOODEN EYE—BARBOSSA'S PIECE OF EIGHT—IS PLACED INTO THE BOWL. . .

"CALYPSO, I RELEASE YOU FROM YOUR HUMAN BONDS!"

CALYPSO, I ASK YOUR FAVOR. SPARE MY SELF, MY SHIP, MY CREW, BUT UNLEASH YOUR *FURY* UPON THOSE WHO DARE PRETEND THEMSELVES YOUR MASTERS, OR MINE!

BUT SUDDENLY, WITH A LAST WORD, CALYPSO TRANSFORMS HERSELF INTO THOUSANDS OF *CRABS* WHICH FALL IN THE SEA AND VANISH. . .

FOOL!

. . . AN ACT WHOSE MEANING IS CLEAR: CALYPSO WILL BE *NO HELP!*

OUR FINAL HOPE HAS FAILED!

HOPE IS NOT LOST! THERE'S STILL A *FIGHT* TO BE HAD.

MEANWHILE, IN THE HAVOC OF THE FIGHTING, JACK BREAKS FREE OF HIS CELL. HE HAS ACHIEVED HIS GOAL: HE IS ABOARD THE *DUTCHMAN*...

FREE!

...AND HE HAS THE *DEAD MAN'S CHEST*!

UNFORTUNATELY, THE *KEY* TO THE CHEST IS IN THE HANDS OF DAVY JONES, WHO KILLED MERCER TO STEAL IT...

HAND IT OVER, SPARROW!

CLANG

GWIIISShh CLANG

CLANG CLANG CLANG CLANG

42

BUT HER BRAVERY PROVIDES DAVY JONES WITH A *HOSTAGE!*

AH, *LOVE!* A STRONG BOND!

JONES!

BRAAAA

HAH! TURNER... YOU MUST HAVE FORGOTTEN...

...I AM TRULY *HEARTLESS!*

TELL ME, WILL TURNER. DO YOU FEAR *DEATH?*

DO YOU?

TU-TUMP

43

JACK. . . YOU ARE A *GOOD* MAN. . .

NO, I'M REALLY NOT!

LET'S FIND OUT!

AAAAH!

WILL!

THE SHOCK OF SEEING HIS SON *MORTALLY WOUNDED* AWAKES BOOTSTRAP BILL FROM THE CURSE THAT FORCED HIM TO OBEY DAVY JONES. . .

WILL! SON!

BOOTSTRAP ATTACKS JONES. . .

YOU WILL DIE FOR THAT

. . . BUT IT ISN'T BOOTSTRAP'S HAND THAT STRIKES THE *FINAL BLOW!*

AAAAH!

JACK KNEW VERY WELL THAT STABBING DAVY JONES'S HEART WOULD HAVE MEANT TAKING HIS PLACE AND LIVING *FOREVER*...

BUT JACK GAVE UP THE ETERNAL LIFE HE WANTED FOR HIMSELF TO LET THE DYING *WILL* STRIKE DOWN DAVY JONES...

...AND BECOME *THE NEW IMMORTAL CAPTAIN* OF THE *FLYING DUTCHMAN!*

AAAAAAAH!

UNFORTUNATELY THIS MEANS THAT WILL CANNOT ABANDON THE *DUTCHMAN* TO FOLLOW JACK AND ELIZABETH BACK TO THE *BLACK PEARL*: THE NEW CAPTAIN MUST STAY ABOARD!

WILL!

AND WHEN BARBOSSA FINALLY GUIDES THE SHIP OUT OF THE TERRIBLE MAELSTROM...

...THE *DUTCHMAN* DISAPPEARS INTO THE *ABYSS OF THE SEA!*

VWWAOOOOOOOSHHHH

THE *ENDEAVOUR* IS *BLOWN AWAY!*

AND AFTER *BECKETT'S DEATH...*

...THE COMPANY FLEET SURRENDERS!

THEY'RE RUNNING OFF!

BUT THERE'S ANOTHER SURPRISE IN STORE: WITH DAVY JONES'S DEATH, THE *DUTCHMAN* AND ITS CREW ARE RESTORED TO THEIR ORIGINAL STATE...

!

...AND A SON HAS HIS FATHER BACK!

I WILL SAIL THE SEAS WITH YOU, IF YOU WILL HAVE ME, *SON!*

YOU'RE WELCOME ABOARD, *FATHER!*